THE Cleanup Surprise

By Christine Loomis

Illustrated by Julie Brillhart

SCHOLASTIC INC.

NEW YORK TORONTO LONDON AUCKLAND SYDNEY

Library of Congress Cataloging-in-Publication Data

Loomis, Christine.
    The cleanup surprise / Christine Loomis; illustrated by
Julie Brillhart.
        p. cm — (My first library)
    Summary: While cleaning up their playground, a class of
preschoolers finds enough useful junk to create a robot.
    ISBN 0-590-49292-6   ISBN 0-590-29264-1 (meets NASTA specifications)
    1. Robots—Fiction. [1. Waste products—Fiction. 2. Stories
in rhyme.] I. Brillhart, Julie, ill. II. Title. III. Series.
PZ8.3.L8619C1 1993
[E]—dc20   92-38735
                              CIP
                              AC

Copyright © 1993 by Scholastic Inc.
Text copyright © 1993 Christine Loomis
Illustrations copyright © 1993 Julie Brillhart
Designed by Bill SMITH STUDIO, Inc.
All rights reserved. Published by Scholastic Inc.
My First Library is a registered trademark of Scholastic Inc.
    4 5 6 7 8 9 10   09   01 00 99 98 97 96 95
Printed in the U.S.A.
First Scholastic printing, 1993

Children, said
Mrs. Klunk one day,
I need your help
Before we play—

To pick up strings
And other things,

Beside the slide,

Beneath the swings,

Along the fence,

Around the tree.
We'll pick up
Everything we see.

We'll check below
The seesaw, too,
To make our playground
Look like new.

Alphonse, Penny,
Amber, Bea,
Michael, Moses,
Jeanmarie,

Rosa, Hattie,
Barry, Bo—
Everyone lined up
To go.

Everyone was
Dressed and ready—
All except, that is,
For Freddy.

Freddy did not
Want to go.
So he lined up
EXTRA slow.

I'm tired of waiting,
Rosa shouted.
Moses frowned,
And Freddy pouted.

Outside, Hattie
Looked around.
A purple pen
Is what she found.

Penny spied
Two paper clips,
A penny, and
Some plastic lips.

Bo helped Harry
Lift a bat,

Rosa searched,

But Fred just sat.

I don't want
To pick up junk.
Why not? It's fun,
Said Mrs. Klunk.

I don't think so,
Freddy said.
He kicked his feet
And sulked instead.

Underneath the
Monkey bars,
Michael spotted
Parts of cars.

Moses, Bea,
And Jeanmarie
Unstuck a bag
Tucked in a tree.

Alphonse sifted
Through the sand.

Amber lent a
Helping hand,
Sorting through the
Tops and caps,
Plastic jacks,
And snaps from straps.

Over, under,
And around,
The class cleaned
Every bit of ground.

Hooray for us!
The playground's neat.
(Not an easy
Cleaning feat!)

It's beautiful,
Said Mrs. Klunk.
Now what to do
With all this junk?

That's a problem,
Rosa said.
And no one spoke,
Except for Fred.

Wheels make eyes,

And here's a cape.
All we need is
Glue and tape.

Amber saw what
Fred saw, too.

Why, here's an arm,

And there's a shoe!

Hattie found a leg
and hat.

Mrs. Klunk gave
Fred a pat.

We're glad you're here
To help us, Fred.
(Freddy turned
A little red.)

All the class
Got busy taping,
Building, gluing,
Painting, shaping,

'Til the project
Was complete.

Gee, they said,
This thing is neat!

And now we know
What junk is for.
Mrs. Klunk, can
We find more?

*For Fran Klunk and all preschool
teachers who nurture and inspire
our children, and for Molly, who
inspires me.   C.L.*